MOLEHOLE MYSTERIES

THE UPSTAIRS CONNECTION

WRITTEN BY
Barbara Davoll
Pictures by Dennis Hockerman

MOODY PRESS
CHICAGO

Moody Press, a ministry of the Moody Bible Institute,
is designed for education, evangelization, and edifi-
cation. If we may assist you in knowing more about
Christ and the Christian life, please write us without
obligation: Moody Press, c/o MLM, Chicago, IL 60610.
Printed in MEXICO.

ISBN: 0-8024-2704-9

Children love the stories of Barbara Davoll, known for her award-winning, best-selling Christopher Churchmouse Classics and now for the Molehole Mystery series. Barbara writes these zany new adventures in Schroon Lake, New York, where she and her husband, Roy, minister at home and abroad with Word of Life International in their Missions Department. Barb manages to stay busy as a wife, mother, grandmother, author, drama teacher, church musician, and homemaker for her husband and Josh, the family Schnauzer.

Illustrator Dennis Hockerman has concentrated on art for children's trade books and textbooks, magazines, greeting cards, and games. He lives with his wife and three children in Mequon, Wisconsin, a suburb of Milwaukee. Mr. Hockerman probably spent more time "underground" than above while developing the characters and creating the etchings for the Molehole Mysteries. Periodically, he would poke his head into his "upstairs connection" to join his family and share with them the adventures of his friends in Molesbury R.F.D.

Contents

THE SICKNESS

It was a cool evening in early fall. The underground home of Dusty and Musty Mole was warmed by a cheery fire that burned brightly in the fireplace. Dusty and Musty, stretched out on the floor, were playing an exciting game of "Shrews and Ladders."

Mother Miranda bustled about her tiny kitchen humming to herself as she fixed earthworm pasta for supper. Father Malcom was due home any minute, and good smells filled their underground burrow.

"Gotcha!" yelled Dusty as he scored heavily to go ahead of his twin in the game.

"Aw, Dusty, you make me sick," complained Musty. "You always get the good cards. You're just lucky."

"Huh!" he responded. "It's skill, sis. Not luck. You're playing with a pro."

Musty stuck out her tongue and reached for a card.

Just then the door opened. "Hi, guys," Father greeted them, hanging his jacket on the coat tree.

The twins looked up and grunted hello, their minds still fixed on winning the game.

Father Malcom walked into the kitchen. "Hello, dear," he said, giving Mother Miranda a hug.

"Oh, Malcom, you're on time. We're just ready to eat. Call the children." Mother dished up the pasta and turned to put the plates on the table.

Her husband sat down at the table with his head in his hands.

"Why, Malcom, what is wrong? Are you all right?" she asked.

Father looked up and nodded wearily. "Yes, Miranda, I'm all right. Just weary and sick at heart. I've come from the home of Murdoch Mole. I saw Dr. Diggerly there. This is the second family in Molesbury this week that has reported a strange illness."

Musty, who had just won the game, followed her nose to the good smells and ambled into the kitchen.

"Did you say something about Murdoch Mole, Dad?" she questioned.

Murdoch's young son, Millard, was a member of the Molehole Mystery Club and a good friend.

"Yes." Father sighed. "Murdoch, his wife, and Millard are very ill. The doctor was just there and has no idea what is causing their sickness. I saw him going in and thought I could be of some help."

Dusty came into the kitchen after putting the game away.

"Well, *pro*, did you get all the pieces put away?" teased Musty. The twins had a rule that the loser always had to put away the stuff.

Dusty nodded and made a face at her. He decided he'd better not brag so much about winning the next time. You really couldn't tell who would win till the game was over.

"Who's sick?" he asked.

Father explained about Murdoch's family.

Dusty was instantly concerned. "What can we do to help?"

"I'll make some earthworm soup after supper and take it over to them," suggested Mother.

"That's a good thought, Mother," said Malcom, "but I'm afraid they are too sick to eat. The doctor is very concerned."

The mole family sat down to eat, but suddenly their appetites were gone. They were very worried about their friends. During supper Father told them of old Moriah Mole, who lived down the street from the Murdoch Moles. He too was very ill, and the doctor said it seemed to be the same kind of illness.

"Maybe it's an *epidermic*," said Musty.

Father and Mother laughed.

"You mean *epidemic*, dear," said Father. "A *hypodermic* is a type of shot a doctor gives to keep you from getting sick. An *epidemic* is when many people get the same kind of illness."

"Whatever." Musty shrugged. "You know what I mean."

"Indeed we do, Musty," said Mother Miranda kindly. "And it may be an epidemic. Did Dr. Diggerly think so, Malcom?"

"He isn't sure." Malcom shook his head. "When you take the earthworm soup to them just ring the bell and leave it on the porch, Miranda. They will understand we don't want to be exposed and perhaps catch their sickness."

"How are they sick?" asked Dusty, who was very worried about his friend Millard.

"They are weak and tired and have no appetite," answered Father Malcom. "Even Murdoch is too weak to be out of bed."

"Is it serious, Father?" asked Musty with her mole eyes open wide.

"Yes, it is, Musty. They have been like this for several days. Old Moriah is in very serious condition."

Just then the doorbell rang. Musty jumped up to answer it.

"Father," she called from the hall. "It's Dr. Diggerly."

Malcom walked into the hallway, wiping his mouth on his napkin.

"Sorry to disturb you, Malcom," the doctor said. "I just wanted to tell you that the Muston Mole family that lives next door to Murdoch is also sick. We're asking that no moles go near their neighborhood until we know what their illness is."

Musty looked at Dusty, who had followed his father into the hall. Her eyes were filled with fear. *Would the mysterious illness threaten all of Molesbury?*

THE CLEANUP CAMPAIGN

The next day the strange illness was the talk of the school.

"I sure hope no one else in our club gets it," said Musty's friend Penney.

"You said it," agreed Musty. "It's too bad about Millard's family. Things have gone so well since the family got back together."

Musty was referring to a time when Millard had run away from home[1] and joined some gypsies. He and his wealthy parents had learned some lessons through that. They now had a wonderful family life.

[1] This story is told in *THE GYPSIES' SECRET*

"Sure would be too bad if they—they—" Penney struggled for words to say what she and Musty were thinking. It would be too bad if they didn't get well.

The bell rang, and the moles all trooped noisily into the classroom. Miss Dugger, the teacher, tapped her ruler on her desk and called them to attention.

"This afternoon we're glad to have Rooto Rabbit speak to us to kick off our Cleanup Campaign," she said and introduced a large brown rabbit.

The rabbit cleared his throat and spoke to them for a few minutes about how important it was for them to keep their world clean.

"We animals can keep our Underground safe and healthy by keeping it free from litter. We need to take care of our garbage properly too."

When the rabbit finished he gave them all litterbags and suggested they fill them and bring them back the next day.

As they left school that evening several members of the Molehole Mystery Club met and headed toward the clubhouse for their weekly meeting.

"We'll have to have a short meeting," said Morty, stooping to pick up a candy wrapper. Otis, his chubby friend, had just thrown it down without thinking.

"Hey, Otis," he called to the chunky mole, who was munching on his candy bar and walking ahead with Dusty. "Put your papers in the litterbag." Morty showed him how.

"Yeah, Morty. I'm sorry. Just forgot."

"You were saying our meeting had to be short," Musty reminded Morty.

"Yeah. So we can get our litterbags full by tomorrow," Morty said.

"The way it looks around here we can fill them up by the time we get to Club," said Penney. She stooped and picked up several candy wrappers and a drink cup that had been thrown carelessly in the roots by the sidewalk.

"Look at *this* mess," called Musty. She had been lagging behind, cleaning up the gutter.

Morty and Penney turned back to help Musty with the trash that had collected near the gutter drain.

"Looks like *pigs* live in Molesbury instead of moles," spat Morty with disgust.

"I've seen you throw stuff down too, Morty," Penney accused him. She and Morty always seemed to be edgy with each other. Penney thought Morty acted like he felt he was better than anyone else.

"That was before I heard Rooto Rabbit," said Morty. "He really made sense with what he said about taking care of our world." Morty wadded up some trash and stuffed it into his litterbag.

"Well, it's true. If we don't take care of it, no one else will," asserted Musty.

Just then Dusty turned and motioned for them to follow him. He turned off the sidewalk onto a seldom-used path that led toward the clubhouse.

"Hey! Why this way, Dusty?" Morty asked.

"Dr. Diggerly said not to go near Murdoch Mole's till they figure out what is making them sick," answered the junior agent.

The moles trooped along, following their leader. It took longer than going by Murdoch Mole's house, but soon the clubhouse was in sight.

As they came up to the shack they saw that Snarkey Mole and Alby Mole were already there. The two stood talking just inside the clubhouse door.

"It's really strange," Alby was saying. "First I heard the crying as I passed by, and then Dr. Diggerly came out of the house."

"What are you talking about?" inquired Dusty as they joined their friends.

Snarkey looked at his fellow club members solemnly. "Dr. Diggerly just told Alby that this afternoon Muston Mole's wife gave birth to a girl mole. The baby mole was born with one leg missing."

The moles looked at each other in shock.

"Poor Muston," said Penney, almost ready to cry. "Didn't Dr. Diggerly say Muston's family had the strange illness too?"

Dusty and Musty nodded.

Then Dusty walked to the front of the clubhouse, and the others followed. "Let's call this meeting to order," he said sadly. "We have something serious to discuss."

THE STRANGE SMELL

Dusty called the meeting of the Molehole Mystery Club to order.

"Today we need to discuss the strange illness that is threatening our town of Molesbury," he said.

"How can we discuss something we know nothing about?" asked Otis. He had finished his candy bar and was noisily licking the chocolate from his fingers.

"You're gross," hissed Musty. Some of Otis' habits disgusted her.

Otis, who secretly liked Musty, looked crushed.

"Musty, will you please not whisper when we are in session?" reminded her brother sharply.

Most of the time Musty responded well to Dusty's leadership. But today she slumped into her seat and stuck out her lip. *He didn't have to embarrass me like that,* she thought.

"It's true we don't know much about this illness," continued Dusty. "But this baby being born with such a problem makes me wonder about it all."

"Can a baby get a sickness before it is born?" asked Penney. She was wondering if the strange illness in the family had caused Muston's baby to be born without a leg.

"I'm not sure," answered Dusty. "I know if a mother takes drugs it can harm the baby."

"Well, that isn't the case with Muston Mole's wife. She is a very fine mother mole and would never do anything to harm herself or her baby," Musty said.

"Sure is funny that all of this is happening in one neighborhood. None of us have caught the illness from Millard, and he's been here with us at Club all the time," Snarkey observed.

"That's right," Mortimer agreed. "And Alby has been helping old Moriah with his yard work each week. He hasn't caught anything from him."

"True," agreed Alby. "Why, I'm healthy as a—as a horse."

They all laughed at the thought of Alby comparing himself to a horse. Although the white albino mole was healthy, he was very small and frail and not at all like a horse.

The hour wore on and still the Club members could not find an explanation for the strange illness. Finally Dusty decided to dismiss the Club for the evening.

"I want all of you to be on the lookout," he said. "There has to be an explanation for all of this. We just have to find it. Our friends' lives may depend on us."

The members looked at him gravely. They all wondered how much time they had to find the answer and who would be the next victim in their little town.

Alby Mole went directly from Club to work at Moriah Mole's. He knew Dr. Diggerly had asked them to stay away from that neighborhood, but he had grown fond of the old gentleman mole who was his employer. Alby looked up to Moriah and thought of him as a father. He couldn't stay away now when Moriah was so ill.

Alby rang the doorbell and waited a long time. At first he was afraid something had happened to Moriah. But then he heard a shuffling of feet.

Old Moriah opened the door just a crack.

"Mr. Moriah," said Alby. "How are you? They said you were sick, and I want to help."

"Oh, Alby, son. You go on along. Don't come in here. They don't know what is wrong with me. I don't want you to catch this awful sickness." Moriah panted weakly.

"But who will help you?" cried Alby. "Someone has to take care of you and cook for you."

"No, Alby. I have no appetite and need nothing. There's nothing anyone can do. Dr. Diggerly has no medicine to help. Please go on now."

Alby kept his foot in the door as Moriah tried to shut it. "I'm staying," said Alby firmly. "I will stay out here and rake. If you need me, call me."

Mr. Moriah shook his head and mumbled sadly. "So like a son to me. But I wish he would go along home."

Because Alby was an orphan and lived alone, the little mole often stayed at Moriah's until dark. Usually Moriah would invite Alby to eat supper with him. The two lonely moles enjoyed being together.

Old Moriah could not see the tears rolling down Alby's face as he raked the yard. *What will I do if something happens to Mr. Moriah?* wondered the little albino.

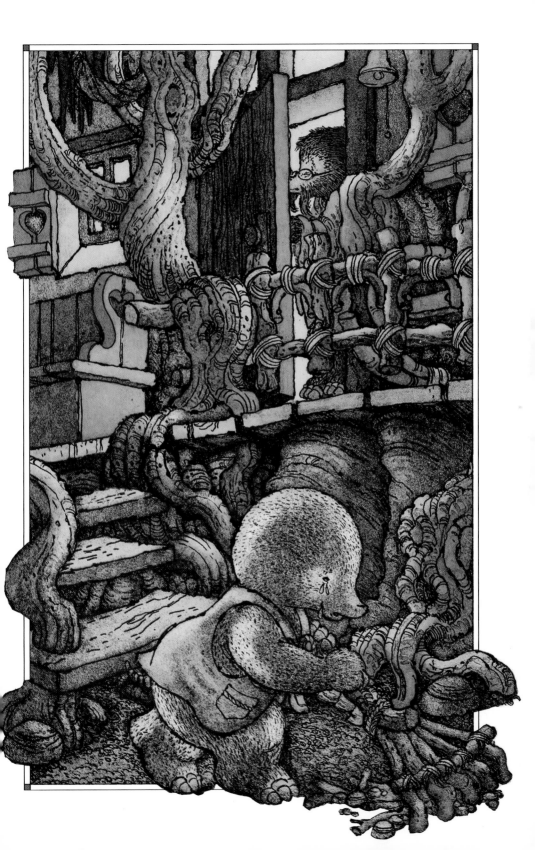

Alby carried a small basket of twigs and roots out behind Moriah's burrow and dumped it. Starting back across the yard, his nose went up in the air. *What is that strange smell?* he wondered.

As he continued raking he noticed the smell in the front yard as well. Alby's pink nose wrinkled in disgust. *That is a terrible smell. No wonder Mr. Moriah is sick if he has to smell that.*

Later that night Alby lay in his bed thinking of Mr. Moriah and the bad smell at his house. *I can't remember ever smelling that before,* he thought. *I wonder if I should report the smell to Dusty?*

SWAMP MOLE MONSTER

The next day at school Alby mentioned to Dusty the strange smell at Moriah's house.

"What were you doing at Moriah's?" stormed the junior agent. "You know Dr. Diggerly told us to stay away from his neighborhood."

"Would you stay away from your father if he were sick?" asked Alby quietly.

Dusty looked at his friend. There were tears in the albino's eyes. Dusty knew how much Mr. Moriah meant to Alby, whose parents had abandoned him.

"I understand, friend," said Dusty. "Now, what's this about a bad smell?"

When Alby told him that he had never noticed the smell before, Dusty looked thoughtful.

"This could be something to look into," he agreed.

"Then let me do it," begged Alby. "I'm over there all the time anyway. Moriah won't let me in because he thinks I'll catch his illness. But I can't stay away. I just work around the outside in case he needs me. I'll see what else I can find out."

"All right," agreed the private detective. "But don't be foolish, Alby. I would stay out of Mr. Moriah's house as much as possible."

Alby nodded. He had high regard for Dusty Mole, who had helped him so much when others were prejudiced against him. He was excited to think that now he might be able to help Dusty discover some clues to help Moriah and the others.

That evening Alby decided to check out the homes of the other families that had the illness.

As he walked between Moriah and Murdoch Mole's homes he noticed the strange smell again. Following his nose he continued on toward Muston Mole's. The smell was there too.

As Alby walked toward the back of Muston Mole's house, the smell grew stronger. Alby was so intent on following his nose that he didn't notice where it was taking him. Behind Muston Mole's house was a path leading off into Withering Roots Swamp.

Alby painfully climbed over the roots and thorns that blocked his path and continued into the swamp. Here the smell grew stronger as he wound his way through the dark tangled mass.

Normally Alby would have stayed miles away from the swamp. It brought back painful memories of the days when he was forced to live there because animals feared him as an albino. Now Alby's excitement grew as he realized he might find an important clue to help his friends.

Suddenly he stepped into a gushy sinkhole. As he fell to his knees the terrible smell seemed to be all around him. The white animal crawled out of the hole and held some of the black mushy goop up to his nose.

Phew! The smell was making him ill. Shaking off the smelly muck, he knew he had to get out of there fast before the smell overpowered him. Darkness was coming on quickly, and the smell was so strong it was making him sick. He was feeling more ill every moment. *I must get out of here,* he thought.

Staggering back the way he came, Alby headed for Muston's house, where he had first entered the swamp. As he came out, he was a strange looking sight. No one would ever have known he was an albino. The white mole was covered with black guck.

Looking down at himself, Alby giggled. *I look like the great Swamp Mole Monster,* he thought. Suddenly dizziness from the smell overwhelmed him. In the darkness he could faintly see Moriah's house across the road. *I'll head there. Moriah surely won't keep me out tonight when he sees me.*

Alby rang Moriah's doorbell and waited for a long time. When his old friend opened the door Alby spoke.

"Mr. Moriah, please let me in. It's Alby."

Moriah took one look and tried to slam the door. He didn't recognize this black mole.

But Alby's foot was in the door. "Please Mr. Moriah. It's me, Alby."

Moriah could hardly believe his ears. Slowly he opened the door again. It was indeed Alby.

"Alby, son. What on earth—? Is that really you?"

Alby weakly pushed himself through the door. "Please help me," he cried. "I'm so weak—"

With that Alby dropped to the floor at his friend's feet. Alby had fainted.

DR. DIGGERLY

When Alby came to he was lying on Moriah's couch. Moriah, although very sick, had somehow managed to clean the guck from his face and body.

"Moriah, I think I know what is making all of you sick," whispered Alby. Weakly he told his friend what he had found and how he himself had felt ill as the smell overpowered him.

"I must get to Dr. Diggerly," said Alby faintly, trying to get up.

"Lie still, son. Dr. Diggerly will be here soon. He comes every evening to check on me."

Alby lay back on the couch. He was too weak to object.

Meanwhile, the Molehole Mystery Club had called an emergency meeting. Dusty explained to the Club members about the smell Alby had detected in Moriah's neighborhood.

"I really thought Alby would be here tonight. He knew I would be sharing this with you," said Dusty, looking worried. "It's just not like him to miss our meeting."

"Maybe Mr. Moriah is worse," suggested Musty.

"That's the only thing I can think of that would keep him away."

Dusty thought for a moment and then made a quick decision. "Snarkey, I want you to get to Dr. Diggerly's house right away. Find out if he knows anything about Moriah. Ask him if he has seen Alby."

"Right," snapped Snarkey, jumping up to leave.

"Get there as fast as you can. The doctor will be going out for his evening calls, and you might miss him."

Snarkey took off for the doctor's house and got there just as the doctor was leaving.

"Dr. Diggerly," panted Snarkey. "Do you know if Mr. Moriah is worse? Alby didn't show up for our Club meeting tonight, and we're wondering if he's with Moriah. We can't go over there because—"

"Because *I told you not to,*" said the doctor. "No, I haven't heard that Mr. Moriah is worse, but I'm on my way there now."

"May I go with you?"

"*Definitely not!*" growled Diggerly. "I don't need any more sick moles around here. I told you to stay away from—"

"Then may I just wait here for you to return? We are really concerned about Alby. He has never missed a meeting of the Molehole Mystery Club."

"I'll be very late," said the doctor.

"That's all right. At least I'll know something."

Dr. Diggerly finally agreed for Snarkey to await his return that night.

Snarkey went back to the clubhouse and told the others he would wait at Dr. Diggerly's for him to return with word about Alby.

Dusty dismissed the Club members, who reluctantly left for their homes. They were all worried about their little albino friend.

Later that night when Dr. Diggerly returned, he found Snarkey fast asleep on the couch in his office.

"Snarkey, wake up! I've news about Alby." Dr. Diggerly shook Snarkey awake. "Your friend Alby is at Moriah's house."

Snarkey jumped up, sleepily rubbing his eyes. "Why did he go there? Is Moriah worse?"

"Calm down, boy. Alby is all right, but I'm afraid he has the illness too."

"Oh, no," groaned Snarkey. "He should never have gone there. Now he has caught the illness from Mr. Moriah."

"He didn't catch the illness from Moriah, son," said Dr. Diggerly. His voice was weary as he sat down heavily on the couch.

"He didn't? Then who did he catch it from?" By this time Snarkey was thoroughly confused.

"I don't think he caught it from anyone," answered the doctor. "I think, from what Alby told me, the illness has something to do with the bad smell coming from the swamp."

Snarky nodded his head sleepily.

"The problem is that anyone who goes into the swamp will get the illness," warned the good doctor.

As Snarkey walked home that night he could not decide what was the best thing to do. Someone had to go into the swamp and find out what was causing the bad smell. Finally he decided that instead of going home he would head for the swamp himself.

Snarkey headed for the wealthy neighborhood of Murdoch and Moriah Mole. As he drew close he could smell the terrible odor. It grew stronger as he walked.

All was dark at Murdoch Mole's mansion. There were no lights at Muston Mole's home either. But lights were blazing at the beautiful old home of Moriah Mole. As Snarkey came close to Moriah's, the door opened and the old gentleman mole came out onto the porch.

Snarkey decided he would ask Mr Moriah about Alby. Just as he started up the walk the old mole hobbled to the steps.

"Who's there?" cried Moriah, peering into the darkness. "Is that you, Snarkey?"

"Yes, Mr. Moriah. It's me," answered Snarkey. "Is everything all right?" He could tell the old mole was very upset.

"No! Everything is not all right. Alby is gone!" cried old Moriah. "He has disappeared!"

RETURN TO THE SWAMP

Snarkey stood staring at Mr. Moriah. *How could Alby be gone?*

"But—but Dr. Diggerly said he had the illness," sputtered Snarkey.

"He does," responded the worried mole. "After Dr. Diggerly left I helped him up the stairs to the guest bedroom. He went to sleep immediately. I just got up to check on him, and he's gone. And he is so sick too."

"Do you have any idea where he could have gone?" asked Snarkey.

"I *know* where he went." said Moriah. "He went back to the swamp to find out more about the bad smell. The doctor thinks that is what is giving us the sickness. I just know that's where he is."

"But how could he go back there when he is so sick?" inquired Snarkey in a worried voice.

"That's just it, Snarkey. He shouldn't be out of bed. He'll faint again and will probably die in there. Oh, woe! My dear little Alby. I might have known he would do this."

The poor old mole staggered to a chair in the hallway and sank into it. Putting his head in his hands he began to weep.

"Mr. Moriah, don't—please don't. I was just on my way there myself to see what I can find out. I'll go after Alby." Snarkey put his arm around the old fellow and patted him awkwardly.

"But you must not. You will get the sickness too! We are all doomed," cried Moriah.

"I am *very strong* and never sick," insisted Snarkey. "Alby is weak and frail because he is an albino. I will be all right. I'll bring him back. Please try not to worry. Let me help you back to bed."

Snarkey assisted Moriah up the steps and tucked him in bed. "Now you try to rest and don't worry. I'll have Alby back here in no time."

With that Snarkey left the upset mole and headed for the swamp. It was just beginning to get daylight.

After nearly an hour of trudging around the swamp Snarkey heard a noise. It was a soft groan.

Moving to the left of where he was standing, he found the huddled form of Alby. The smell was all around them. It was so strong that Snarkey felt dizzy.

Quickly he knelt over his friend. "Alby! It's me, Snarkey. Are you all right?"

"Snarkey?" whispered Alby faintly. "You have to get out of here. This stuff is bad. It will make you sick. Get away, please."

"Not without you, my friend," said Snarkey. "Have you found the source of this bad smell?"

Alby nodded his head. "It's over there. I found a long root of some kind. The smell is coming from it."

Snarkey took off his jacket and gently laid Alby's head on it. He then moved in the direction Alby had pointed. Suddenly he tripped. Then, crawling along on his hands and knees, he could feel something hard, long, and smooth.

This is no root, thought Snarkey. *I don't know what it is, but it isn't a root. It feels like a piece of metal.*

Snarkey suddenly realized that the long piece of metal was coming from the Upstairs. The Upstairs was what the moles always called the aboveground, where the humans lived. Snarkey hurried back to Alby.

"I don't know what it is, Alby, but I think it's a piece of metal coming from the Upstairs. I'll have to come back with Dusty. But now I must get you out of here."

Snarkey picked up his ill friend and began to climb over the tangled mass in the swamp. It was hard going, especially since he felt so weak from the smell. But eventually he emerged from the swamp and carried the white animal to Moriah's house.

Opening the door was a trick while still holding Alby. But Snarkey didn't want to disturb Mr. Moriah. Finally managing to get in the door, he started up the stairs carrying Alby.

They were met at the top of the steps by the old mole in his dressing gown.

"Is he all right?" cried Moriah fearfully.

"He's very sick, but he's alive," said Snarkey. "I'll get the doctor right away."

Soon they had Alby tucked into bed.

Snarkey wasn't feeling well himself, but he started for the doctor's house. Several times he had to sit down and rest because he was so dizzy. But eventually he reached Dr. Diggerly's.

As soon as Dr. Diggerly heard what had happened, he left for Moriah's home.

Snarkey headed for his own home and bed. Walking along slowly toward his burrow, he thought about the situation. *What is the bad stuff?* he wondered. *And how can we stop it from coming into the Underground?* The problem seemed hopeless to the young exhausted mole.

THE UPSTAIRS PIPE

Later that afternoon Snarkey reported all the events of the past night to the Molehole Mystery Club.

Dusty was the first to speak after hearing Snarkey's report. "We must do something about this immediately. I heard on the way here that another family on Moriah's street has the illness. It will soon be all over Molesbury."

Snarkey agreed. "The smell is getting stronger all the time. Now you can smell it several blocks away. The animals living there will be getting sick next."

"If Snarkey can go into the swamp for a short while and not be overcome, I'm sure I can too," said Dusty.

"I'll go with you," volunteered Mortimer.

"All right. Let's tie something around our noses so we can't smell the stuff so strongly. Otis, I want you to keep watch at the entrance to the swamp. Don't allow anyone in. Make a big sign saying it is dangerous in there."

"Right," said Otis.

"What can *we* do?" asked Musty. She and Penney always wanted to be involved in anything that was happening.

"We'll assign you to the nursing detail," said her brother. "Now that we know this illness is not catching, you can go to each of the homes and help them in any way that you can."

"I'm so glad it's not an epidermic—uh, *epidemic*," she said, correcting her pronunciation of the big word she had just learned.

They all laughed as they left the clubhouse. They felt encouraged to know more about the sickness. If they had known what lay ahead they wouldn't have laughed.

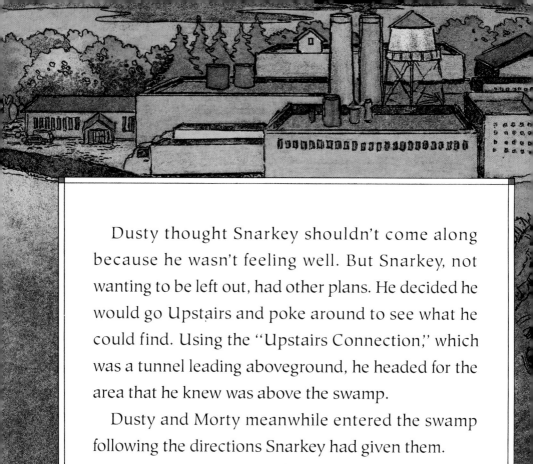

Dusty thought Snarkey shouldn't come along because he wasn't feeling well. But Snarkey, not wanting to be left out, had other plans. He decided he would go Upstairs and poke around to see what he could find. Using the "Upstairs Connection," which was a tunnel leading aboveground, he headed for the area that he knew was above the swamp.

Dusty and Morty meanwhile entered the swamp following the directions Snarkey had given them.

"Here it is, Dusty!" cried Morty. "It's a root of some kind!" He had tripped over the piece of metal that Snarkey had described.

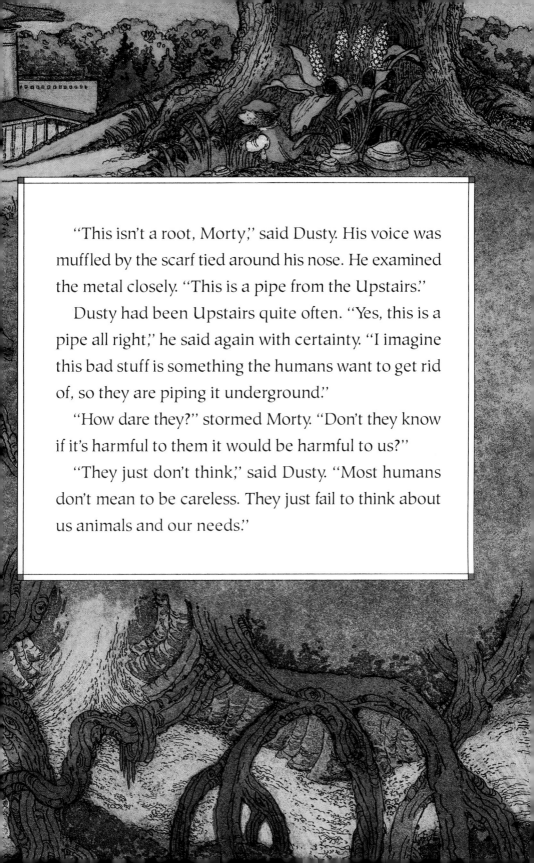

"This isn't a root, Morty," said Dusty. His voice was muffled by the scarf tied around his nose. He examined the metal closely. "This is a pipe from the Upstairs."

Dusty had been Upstairs quite often. "Yes, this is a pipe all right," he said again with certainty. "I imagine this bad stuff is something the humans want to get rid of, so they are piping it underground."

"How dare they?" stormed Morty. "Don't they know if it's harmful to them it would be harmful to us?"

"They just don't think," said Dusty. "Most humans don't mean to be careless. They just fail to think about us animals and our needs."

"What will we do about it?" cried Morty. He was starting to feel sick even though they had their noses covered.

"Well, first let's see where this pipe is leading." Using his strong front feet, which were just like shovels, Dusty began to dig up through the ground.

As Morty helped, the dirt began to fly.

Suddenly Dusty yelled. "What in the world—" He had hold of something furry. It was an animal's leg.

From aboveground they could hear the animal. "Hey! Let go of my leg!"

Dusty let go. With a few more pawfuls of dirt he crawled through the earth to the Upstairs.

Standing in front of him was a startled Snarkey.

"Snarkey! You scared me to death! What were you doing?"

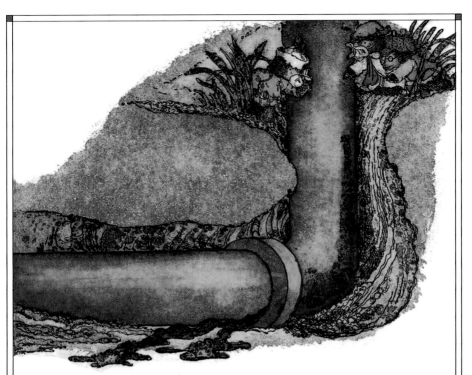

By this time Morty had crawled out of the hole and stood staring at their fellow Club member.

"I came up here to see what I could find. I figured this spot was right above the bad smell, so I started digging too. Did you find the metal thing?"

"We did," answered Dusty. "It's a pipe, and it's coming from up here. See?" A few more digs in the earth revealed the pipe that had been buried in the ground.

Snarkey gave a low whistle when he saw the pipe.

"Where are we?" asked Dusty looking around.

"This is a big factory up here," said Snarkey. "I've already found out they make some kind of chemicals."

"Must be bad stuff," observed Morty. "Look over there." He pointed to a large smokestack rising above the factory. Black smelly smoke was pouring from the large chimney.

"Phew! How can the humans stand this stuff?" wondered Snarkey.

"Dusty," suggested Morty, "there's a lake over there with a beaver lodge. Let's call on our beaver friends and see what they can tell us."

CLEAVER BEAVER

Snarkey, Dusty, and Morty walked around the lake for a time, but saw no activity in the beaver lodge. It seemed to be abandoned. There were no trees that showed beavers had been chewing on them.

"Looks like they've moved out," said Snarkey. "Probably couldn't take the smell coming out of that chimney."

"Well, they've either moved away or the stuff has killed them," said Dusty sadly.

"Dusty, over here," called Morty from the other side of the little lake.

Dusty scuttled over to see. Morty was kneeling beside something in the water. A dead beaver floated among the weeds growing along the edge of the lake.

"What a sadness," said the junior agent. "This is a very unhealthy place."

"Why don't we go over to Beaver Creek?" suggested Snarkey. "I know the beavers over there. Perhaps they will know more about this."

Beaver Creek was a beehive of activity. A sound like a buzz saw greeted them. The beavers were working at their lumber business.

Snarkey found his friend Cleaver Beaver, who was glad for an excuse to rest awhile. Cleaver's nephews, Grinder and Bo, also stopped their chopping to talk to the moles.

Dusty explained their problem and how they had found the abandoned beaver lodge.

"It's really too bad," said Cleaver. "Several beavers died there before they realized what was happening. When they realized their lake was polluted they moved away."

"What's wrong with the humans?" cried Mortimer indignantly. "Don't they see what they're doing by dumping this bad stuff?"

"They must," said Bo. "Even the humans are getting bad diseases from it. But I guess they have to get rid of it some way."

"Well, we have to do something or the whole Underground will be polluted," said Dusty. "Surely their police will do something."

"They would if they know about it. But how can we tell them? We don't speak their language," observed Snarkey.

"Hmm," said Dusty.

Dusty's friends looked at the junior agent. He had a look on his face that they recognized. He was forming a plan.

"Would you beavers be willing to help us?" he asked.

The beavers agreed to do so as long as it didn't keep them from their work too long. They were busy building their winter lodges.

"Suppose we were to flood the road leading to the factory?" suggested Dusty. "The police would have to come in and do something then. If we could expose the pipe, perhaps they would discover the mess and make the factory clean it up."

Quickly the animals formed their plans. The beavers would go to the polluted lake and build a dam so that the lake would overflow and close the road. They thought if they changed workers every hour none of them would get sick.

Grinder left to enlist more beaver help. The moles went back to the pipe and began to expose it so that the police would find it. Soon the pipe was entirely out in the open.

"Now all we have to do is let the beavers do their work," said Morty, dusting himself off.

Later that night the beaver construction crew began its work. By morning an incredible amount of building had been done.

"One more night of work, and we should have it done," said Cleaver. He was a funny sight with a rag tied around his nose and wearing a lumberjack outfit

and a hard hat.

The next morning the construction work was finished.

"Looks like we're just in time for a good rainstorm," said Cleaver.

Dusty looked at the sky. Huge black clouds threatened, and thunder began to roll. The animals headed for cover under some trees as heavy rain began to fall. They watched as the rain poured and filled the polluted lake. Water spilled over the bank and ran toward the area where the pipe was located.

"Look, Dusty!" cried Cleaver. "There's one last thing our poor beaver friend can do for us."

The dead beaver from the polluted lake was being carried along with the flood waters. Cleaver ran from his cover and threw some branches near the exposed pipe. The dead beaver came to rest right beside the pipe.

"Now they'll be sure to find the pipe," said the drenched Cleaver, shaking the rain from his fur.

All the animals could do now was wait.

THE FLOOD

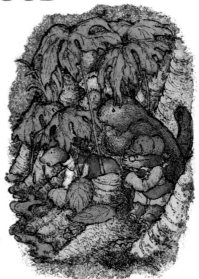

As the animals watched from their cover, the blinding rainstorm continued all day. It was flooding the road to the factory.

"It will soon be time for the factory workers to stop work for the night," said Morty. "If they don't leave soon they won't be able to get to their cars." The flood was fast approaching the factory parking lot.

"There's the quitting whistle now," cried Snarkey.

The factory workers began to rush from the building toward the parking lot. Some were wading up to their ankles in the fast rising water.

The last car to leave the parking lot stalled in the water. The driver left it standing and ran toward another car that had made it through. He jumped into that car, and they got out just in time. The parking lot now looked like a lake.

"This is really some storm," yelled Dusty above the sound of the rushing water. "Who would have thought such a rain would come just when we needed it."

"I'm heading for Beaver Creek," cried Cleaver. "You won't need us anymore."

After many thanks from the moles, the beavers swam through the flood waters toward their home.

Snarkey laughed to see the beavers swimming down the road. "They may be able to swim all the way to Beaver Creek," he said with a giggle.

Dusty chuckled. "That will suit them just fine."

"I wish we were snug and dry underground," complained Morty. The rain was running off his body in little streams.

"I'm not going home till I see what happens up here," Dusty said. "Let's move up on that bank to higher ground."

The three animals headed for a large tree that grew on a high bank. Overlooking the lake, they could have a good view of all that went on.

Through the long night the rain poured. The moles made a shallow burrow under the tree. They were able to dry out in there and find a few earthworms to eat for supper. Finally they curled up together and slept as the storm raged over their heads.

The next morning when they awoke the rain had stopped. Dusty poked his nose out of their temporary home and breathed deeply. The awful smell that had been in the Underground was all around them.

"I hope the police come soon," he called back to the other two moles. "The drains and sewers are all plugged up, and the smell is aboveground now." From the burrow door he could see the dead beaver still caught between the branches by the pipe.

Just as Morty and Snarkey came out of the burrow, a sound startled the three moles.

"That sounds like a truck," said Morty.

"It had better not be," Snarkey responded. "Nothing can get through this water."

"You're wrong, Snarkey," observed Dusty. "Look! It's a boat!"

The moles watched in amazement as a police boat came into view, cruising slowly. Two policemen and a man with a camera were in the boat. The boat cruised along as the man with the camera took pictures of the factory standing with water all around it.

"Watch!" cried Dusty with excitement. "They're coming this way!"

The boat turned and came toward the area
where the pipe and the dead beaver were. One of the
policemen stood and pointed toward the beaver. The
man with the camera took many pictures of the beaver
and the pipe. The animals could hear the three men
talking excitedly.

"I wish we could understand what they are saying,"
said Morty.

"I do too," agreed Dusty. "Look! They're tying their
handkerchiefs around their noses. It's for sure they
don't like the smell either."

The policeman driving the boat brought it up close
to the pipe. The other policeman reached from the boat
and tugged on the pipe to see where it came from.
The cameraman took a couple more pictures, and then
the boat sped off toward the nearby town.

"Let's hope they know the bad stuff from the factory
is causing the smell." Morty sounded worried.

"They know all right," said Dusty.

Then the animals saw some dead mice and a squirrel
floating in the water.

"Morty, you and Snarkey go into the woods and
warn the animals. Tell them not to come near this place
or drink this water. Tell them it's polluted."

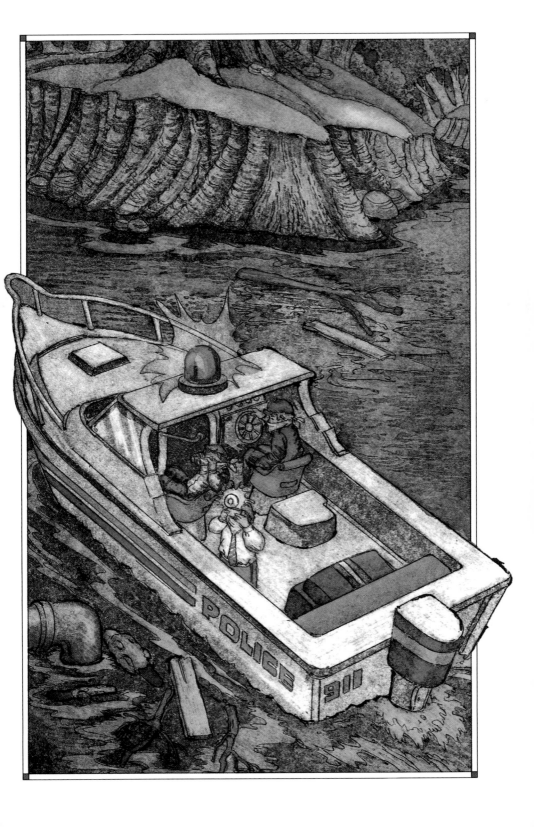

As Snarkey and Morty left, Dusty continued watching the flood. He had to go inside the burrow several times to keep from becoming sich from the terrible smell.

In a short while more men in boats arrived. They were dressed in strange outfits and wore masks over their faces.

I guess those masks allow them to breathe clean air, thought Dusty with admiration. *Men are really smart. You'd think they'd be smart enough not to make such bad stuff. Humans are sure hard to figure out sometimes.*

Workmen wearing the funny outfits swarmed around the lake. Taking a boat to the center of the lake, they began to tear apart the dam the beavers had built. When the dam was torn apart, the flood waters began to go down. Soon Dusty could see the road and the parking lot.

Other workmen wearing masks worked over by the exposed pipe. Dusty noticed that the dead beaver was gone. Workmen in boats skimmed the water picking up all the floating trash.

By evening the workers were able to enter the factory. The flood was over, and they could open the doors. Lights went on in all the offices. Men with briefcases came and went. They had serious expressions on their faces.

Snarkey and Morty returned from warning the woodland animals. "I think the smell is getting better," observed Snarkey.

"Maybe the factory has stopped sending the bad stuff through the pipe," Morty suggested.

"Look!" cried Dusty.

An important looking man he recognized was entering the factory carrying a briefcase. Two other men were with him. One of them pointed toward the pipe.

"That's the mayor of the town," said the junior agent excitedly. "Maybe he will make the factory stop using the bad stuff."

It was suppertime, and the little moles were tired and hungry.

"Let's go home, boys," said Dusty heading toward the Upstairs Connection that led underground. "The humans will have to deal with this in their own way. We've done all we can do."

"SHREWS AND LADDERS"

When Dusty reached his burrow there was a lot of excitement there. As he entered his dugout home, Musty came rushing downstairs carrying a tray full of dirty dishes.

"Dusty's home!" she called, bustling toward the kitchen.

Penney clattered down the stairs behind her carrying another tray of dishes.

Setting the tray down quickly Musty rushed into the hall to give her brother a welcome hug.

"What's up?" asked Dusty.

"Mother and Penney and I are nursing all the sick moles. We brought them here to get them away from the bad smell. As soon as we got them out of that neighborhood they began to improve."

Musty tied an apron around her waist and drew some steaming dishwater. "Here, Penney. You dry," she directed, handing her friend a towel.

Beginning to wash the empty dishes Musty said, "It's a lot of work, being a nurse. But it's fun. We're really enjoying it. Did you guys discover anything aboveground?"

"Sure did," answered her twin.

Just then the doorbell rang.

"That's probably Dr. Diggerly," said Musty. "Let him in, will you, Penney?"

Dr. Diggerly went immediately to the patients' rooms. When he came downstairs later he was very pleased.

"All of the animals are doing very well," he announced. "Musty and Penney and Mother Miranda are doing a fine job running this hospital."

Penney and Musty beamed.

Mother Miranda bustled into the kitchen. "I'm just going to fix supper, Doctor. You must stay and eat with us. I'm sure we all want to hear about Dusty's trip to the Upstairs."

When the Malcom Mole family finally sat down to eat, not only Dr. Diggerly joined them but Alby Mole as well. The doctor said he thought Alby was almost fully recovered.

"Well, Doctor, it surely is good news that all of our friends are recovering so nicely," said Malcom between bites of turnip green salad.

The fine doctor chuckled. "Even old Moriah is about to turn handstands up there. A couple more days and they will all be fit as fiddles."

"Now Dusty, tell us what happened aboveground." Father Malcom turned to hear his son.

Dusty told with pleasure all that had happened Upstairs. The moles were pleased to know that the humans had been alerted to the bad problem being caused by the factory.

"Do you think they will stop using that bad stuff?" asked Mother Miranda. "Our friends must not go back to their homes until it is safe."

"I'm sure they will, Mother. Snarkey and I plan to go Upstairs again tomorrow and see about it," Dusty assured her.

A pleasant evening around the fire followed as Dusty told about their beaver friends and the men with the funny outfits. When the doctor looked in on his patients later, they were all sleeping soundly.

The next day as Snarkey and Dusty approached the factory, they saw many changes. The pipe leading to the Underground was gone. The flood waters were also gone. The most striking change, however, was the smokestack. Workers on a high platform were tearing the smokestack down.

"What do you think, Dusty?" asked Snarkey. "It looks as though they won't be using that smokestack anymore."

"Sure looks like it to me," agreed Dusty. Lifting his nose he took a deep smell. "It's starting to smell better up here already."

Snarkey inhaled deeply too. "You're right. They must have stopped using the bad stuff."

That evening the *Underground Gazette,* Molesbury's newspaper, had a front page article about the big cleanup aboveground. There was a picture of Dusty, Snarkey, and Morty and another picture of Dr. Diggerly and Alby Mole.

Father Malcom sat in front of the fire reading the paper. Mother Miranda was knitting. Dusty and Musty were playing their favorite game again, "Shrews and Ladders."

Father Malcom looked over his spectacles at his son, who was sprawled out in front of the gameboard. "Your picture is here on the front page, Dusty. Looks like you're a hero, son."

"Uh-huh," mumbled the boy mole absent-mindedly. "It takes one to beat my sister."

Musty looked up at her brother. "You're always a hero to me." Her eyes twinkled. "But that doesn't mean you're a winner." Triumphantly she laid the winning card on the matching space.

Dusty sighed. Somehow his sister always had the winning card. "I'll put the game away," he said with a playful pout.

"And I'll help you," said his twin agreeably. "You're a pretty nice loser."

Father Malcom and Mother Miranda smiled at each other. Usually they were glad they had twin moles. Tonight was one of those times.

THROUGH THE SPYGLASS

What a time the animals in Molesbury had with that terrible odor from the factory Upstairs. Sometimes humans *are* hard to understand.

Take a look through my spyglass now to see how Dusty and his friends are doing. The factory that was sending the bad stuff through the pipe was ordered to stop making the terrible smelling substance. The mayor and other officials made sure that this was done.

After a time the park and woods around the factory were once again safe for all of the animals and humans. The polluted lake was cleaned up and became crystal clear again. Eventually a new beaver family moved to the lake and began cutting trees to build their lodge.

Dusty and his friends were relieved that there was no longer a problem in the Underground with the terrible smell. Moriah Mole, the Murdoch Mole family, and Muston Mole's family all recovered nicely. The little baby mole that was born without a leg has learned to adjust. Still it is sad to see her and know she is crippled because of the bad smell.

The humans Upstairs have learned how dangerous it can be to dump waste material. Many humans are active now in clean-air campaigns.

The Cleanup Campaign at Molesbury Elementary School becomes bigger every year. More and more moles realize how important it is to take care of the earth.

The Word of God tells us in Nehemiah 9:6, "You alone are the Lord. You made the heavens…the earth and all that is on it. You gave life to everything."

It is important for us to realize that since God made the earth and gave it to us, we have a responsibility to take care of it. That means the way we care for our trash. That means the way we use the resources the Lord has given us, such as light and energy. We can please the Lord by caring for what He has given us.

Are you a caring citizen here on God's earth? Remember, if *you* don't care for our earth, who will?

UNDERGROUND "DIG-TIONARY"

BEAVER (bē´-ver): A large aquatic rodent of the genus Castor family with thick fur, a flat paddlelike tail, and chisellike front teeth *(Webster's New Collegiate Dictionary).*

Beavers are some of the most interesting animals you will ever know. They do some of the most fascinating things. For instance:

Did you know that beavers always slap their tails when they are in danger? This is a language that is well understood in the beaver world. They come running to help each other when they hear this sound.

Did you know that beavers usually work at night? They can construct an entire beaver dam in one night. Sometimes they can be seen during the day too, but they are mostly nocturnal (night) animals.

Did you know that beavers build the bottom part of their beaver lodges out of wood they like to eat? They build the upper story of their lodge of wood they don't prefer to eat. In this way they "eat themselves out of house and home" during the winter. They have all of their food right there in their lodge and don't have to work during the cold months.

Did you know that beavers spend at least two hours a day grooming themselves and each other? They are very clean animals.

Did you know that working beavers grind their teeth constantly to sharpen them? In this way their teeth act like a very sharp buzz saw.

Did you know that beavers build tunnels in the riverbanks close to their lodges? They have feeding chambers back in these tunnels, where they enjoy their food.

Did you know that beavers make good pets? They have been known to live in homes with people for many years. They can be trained to use a litter box just like a cat. Sometimes they even have been known to sleep with their owners.

Wouldn't you like to meet Cleaver Beaver?

JOIN
MOLEHOLE MYSTERY
CLUB

Would you like to join the Molehole Mystery Club? This will entitle you to receive your very own Molehole Mystery Club ID card and Dusty's free newsletter. The newsletter will be filled with clues and mysteries you can solve and lots of fun things to do.

The newsletter will share things with you from God's Word that will help you live a happy life as a child of God. My spyglass shows me some wonderful words from the Bible that you need to remember always.

These verses are the Molehole Mystery Club Motto, and you will need to memorize them to become a member. The words are found in the Bible [1 Thessalonians 5:21 and 22]: "Test everything. Hold on to the good. Avoid [stay away from] every kind of evil" *(New International Version)*.

We'll be looking for your membership application for our club. See you in the next Molehole adventure story. Happy reading!